DISCARDED BY
SAYVILLE LIBRARY

NBA CHAMPIONS: MILWAUKEE BUCKS

AARON FRISCH

CREATIVE EDUCATION

Published by Creative Education
P.O. Box 227, Mankato, Minnesota 56002
Creative Education is an imprint of The Creative Company
www.thecreativecompany.us

Book and cover design by Blue Design (www.bluedes.com)
Art direction by Rita Marshall
Printed by Corporate Graphics in the United States of America

Photographs by december.com (John December), Getty Images (Brian Babineau/NBAE, Vernon Biever/NBAE, Vernon Biever/WireImage, Gary Dineen/NBAE, Focus On Sport, Walter Iooss Jr./NBAE, Heinz Kluetmeier/Sports Illustrated, Ronald C. Modra/Sports Imagery, Dick Raphael/NBAE)

Copyright © 2012 Creative Education
International copyright reserved in all countries. No part of this book may be reproduced in any form without written permission from the publisher.

Library of Congress Cataloging-in-Publication Data

Frisch, Aaron.
Milwaukee Bucks / by Aaron Frisch.
p. cm. — (NBA champions)
Includes bibliographical references and index.
Summary: A basic introduction to the Milwaukee Bucks professional basketball team, including its formation in 1968, great players such as Lew Alcindor, championship, and stars of today.
ISBN 978-1-60818-138-4
1. Milwaukee Bucks (Basketball team)—History—Juvenile literature. I. Title.
GV885.52.M54.F75 2011
796.323'64'0977595—dc22   2010051575

CPSIA: 030111 PO1448

First edition
9 8 7 6 5 4 3 2 1

Cover: Andrew Bogut
Page 2: Brandon Jennings
Right: Kareem Abdul-Jabbar (far right)
Page 6: Andrew Bogut

TABLE OF CONTENTS

Welcome to Milwaukee 9

Bucks History 11

Why Are They Called the Bucks? 15

Bucks Facts 16

Bucks Stars 19

Glossary 24

Index 24

The Bucks have played in the Bradley Center since 1988

Milwaukee is a city in Wisconsin. Milwaukee is one of the snowiest cities in the United States in the winter. It has an **arena** called the Bradley Center that is the home of a basketball team called the Bucks.

Milwaukee usually gets about 52 inches of snow in the winter

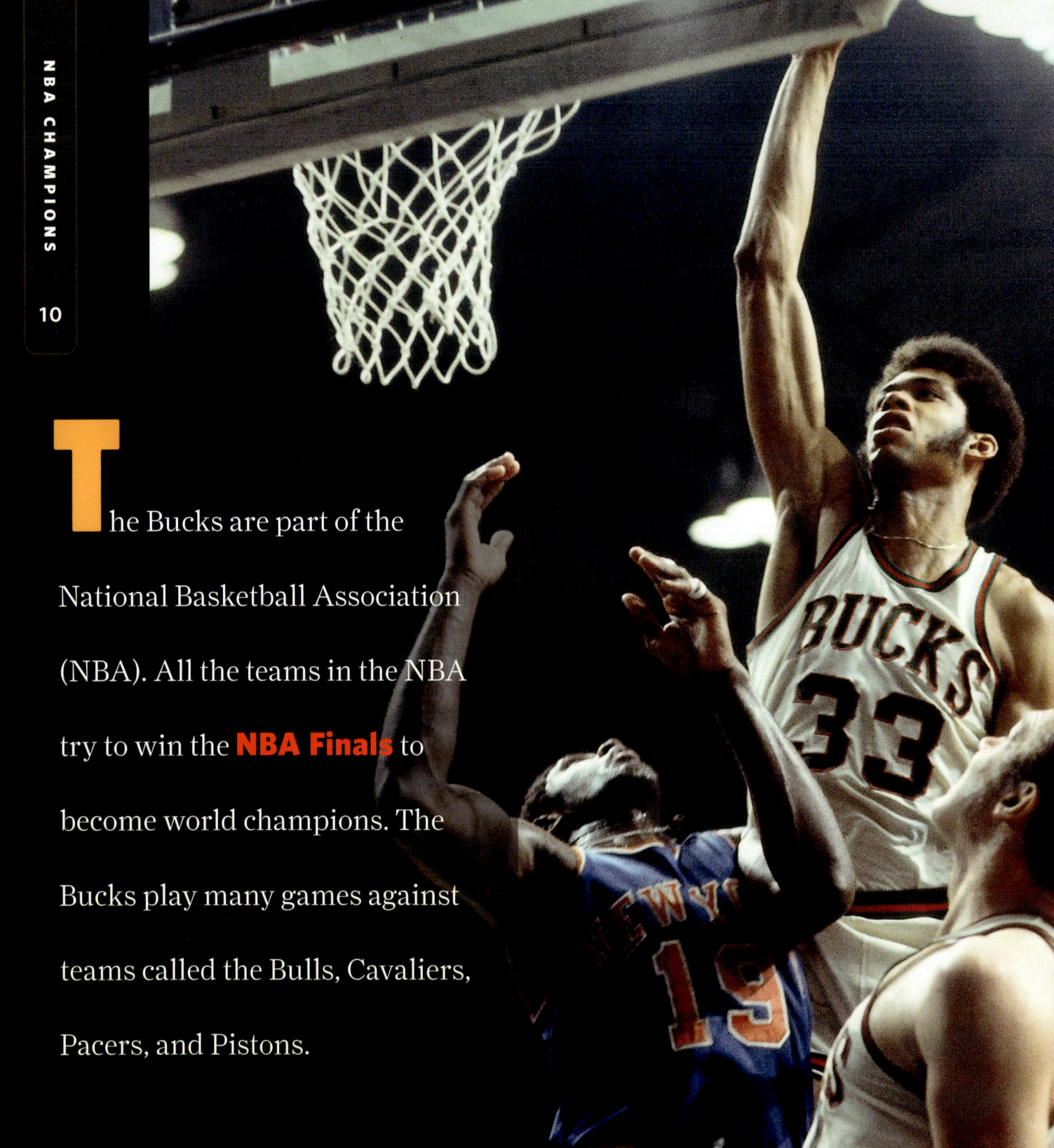

NBA CHAMPIONS 10

The Bucks are part of the National Basketball Association (NBA). All the teams in the NBA try to win the **NBA Finals** to become world champions. The Bucks play many games against teams called the Bulls, Cavaliers, Pacers, and Pistons.

MILWAUKEE BUCKS

11

The Bucks started playing in 1968. In 1969, Milwaukee got a 7-foot-2 center named Lew Alcindor. (Later, he changed his name to Kareem Abdul-Jabbar.) He scored many points with his **hook shot**.

SAY IT LIKE THIS

Lew Alcindor
LOO al-SIN-der

Lew Alcindor

In 1971, Alcindor and **swingman** Oscar Robertson led the Bucks to the NBA Finals. They beat the Baltimore Bullets in four straight games to win the championship in just their third season! No other NBA team had ever won a championship that quickly.

SAY IT LIKE THIS
Kareem Abdul-Jabbar
kuh-REEM ab-DOOL juh-BAR

MILWAUKEE BUCKS

13

NBA fans called Milwaukee star Oscar Robertson "The Big O"

NBA CHAMPIONS 14

Swingman Marques Johnson played for the Bucks from 1977 to 1984

The Bucks had many good seasons after that. Coach Don Nelson helped them get to the **playoffs** a lot in the 1980s. But Milwaukee could not win another championship.

Why Are They Called the Bucks?
A buck is a male deer. There are many deer in the woods of Wisconsin. Bucks grow large antlers and can run fast and jump high.

Coach Don Nelson

BUCKS FACTS

- **Started playing:** 1968
- **Conference/division:** Eastern Conference, Central Division
- **Team colors:** green, red, and white
- **NBA championship:**
  1971 — 4 games to 0 versus Washington Bullets
- **NBA Web site for kids:** http://www.nba.com/kids/

In 2001, fast guard Ray Allen led the Bucks to the playoffs. They had to beat the Philadelphia 76ers in only one more game to get to the NBA Finals. But they lost.

Ray Allen helped make the Bucks a high-scoring team from 1996 to 2003

Bucks stars Bob Lanier (above) and Sidney Moncrief (opposite)

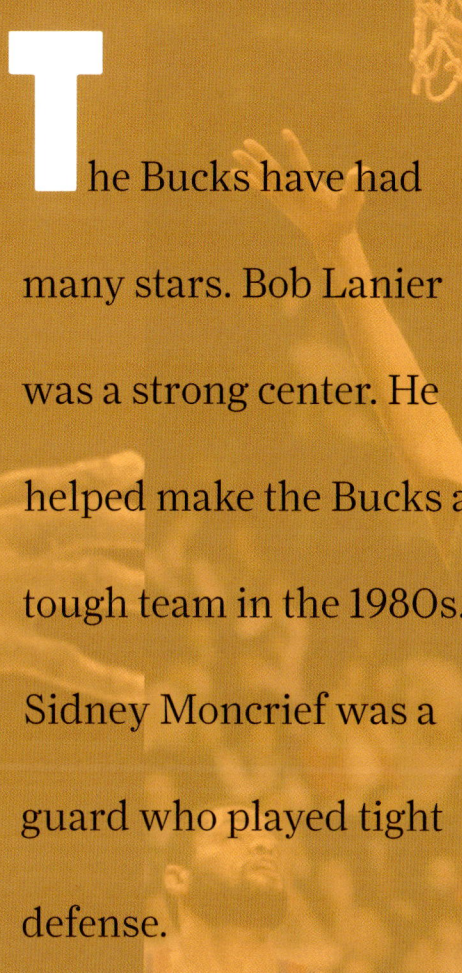

The Bucks have had many stars. Bob Lanier was a strong center. He helped make the Bucks a tough team in the 1980s. Sidney Moncrief was a guard who played tight defense.

SAY IT LIKE THIS

Lanier
luh-NEER

NBA CHAMPIONS

20

Glenn Robinson spent his first eight NBA seasons in Milwaukee

Glenn Robinson joined Milwaukee in 1994. He was a high-scoring forward nicknamed "Big Dog." Andrew Bogut was another Bucks star. He was a center from Australia who threw slick passes.

Andrew Bogut was good at passing, rebounding, and blocking shots

In 2009, the Bucks added Brandon Jennings. He was a quick point guard who scored 55 points in 1 game his first season! That was a new team **record**. Milwaukee fans hoped that he would help lead the Bucks to their second NBA championship!

By 2011, Brandon Jennings was the top scorer for the Bucks

MILWAUKEE BUCKS

23

GLOSSARY

arena — a large building for indoor sports events; it has many seats for fans

hook shot — a shot where a player turns sideways and shoots with just one hand

NBA Finals — a series of games between two teams at the end of the playoffs; the first team to win four games is the champion

playoffs — games that the best teams play after a season

record — something that is the most or best ever

swingman — a basketball player who can play as a guard or forward

INDEX

Alcindor, Lew	11, 12
Allen, Ray	16
Bogut, Andrew	20
Bradley Center	9
Jennings, Brandon	22
Lanier, Bob	19
Moncrief, Sidney	19
NBA championship	12, 16
NBA Finals	10, 12, 16
Nelson, Don	15
playoffs	15, 16
Robertson, Oscar	12
Robinson, Glenn	20
team name	15
team record	22

Sayville Library
88 Greene Avenue
Sayville, NY 11782

JUL 15 2013